tiger tales

an imprint of ME Media, LLC

5 River Road, Suite 128, Wilton, CT 06897

Published in the United States 2013

Originally published in Great Britain 2012

by Hodder Children's Books

a division of Hachette Children's Books

Text copyright © 2012 Gillian Shields

Illustrations copyright © 2012 Cally Johnson-Isaacs

CIP data is available

ISBN-13: 978-1-58925-126-7

ISBN-10: 1-58925-126-1

Printed in China

12CB2412

For more insight and activities,

visit us at www.tigertalesbooks.com

For my darling daughter, my lovely Sasha G.S.

For Dad with love C.J.

Elephantantrum!

by Gillian Shields

Illustrated by Cally Johnson-Isaacs

tiger tales

Ellie had **everything**.

But she wanted more. She wanted an elephant.

She wouldn't eat or sleep or brush her hair.
She wouldn't smile or play or do her homework.
She wouldn't even get out of bed until she
got what she wanted.

"Please get up, Ellie," said her father.
"NO!" she replied. "Not until you get me an ELEPHANT!"

Ellie's father went to his big fancy office.

He wrote letters and made phone calls.

He worked and worried and fussed and fretted until . . .

an elephant arrived for Ellie.

Ellie jumped up and down in excitement. She couldn't wait to boss her new elephant around.

"Come here, Elephant!" she said. "Give me a ride! Do a trick! Pick up my toys!"

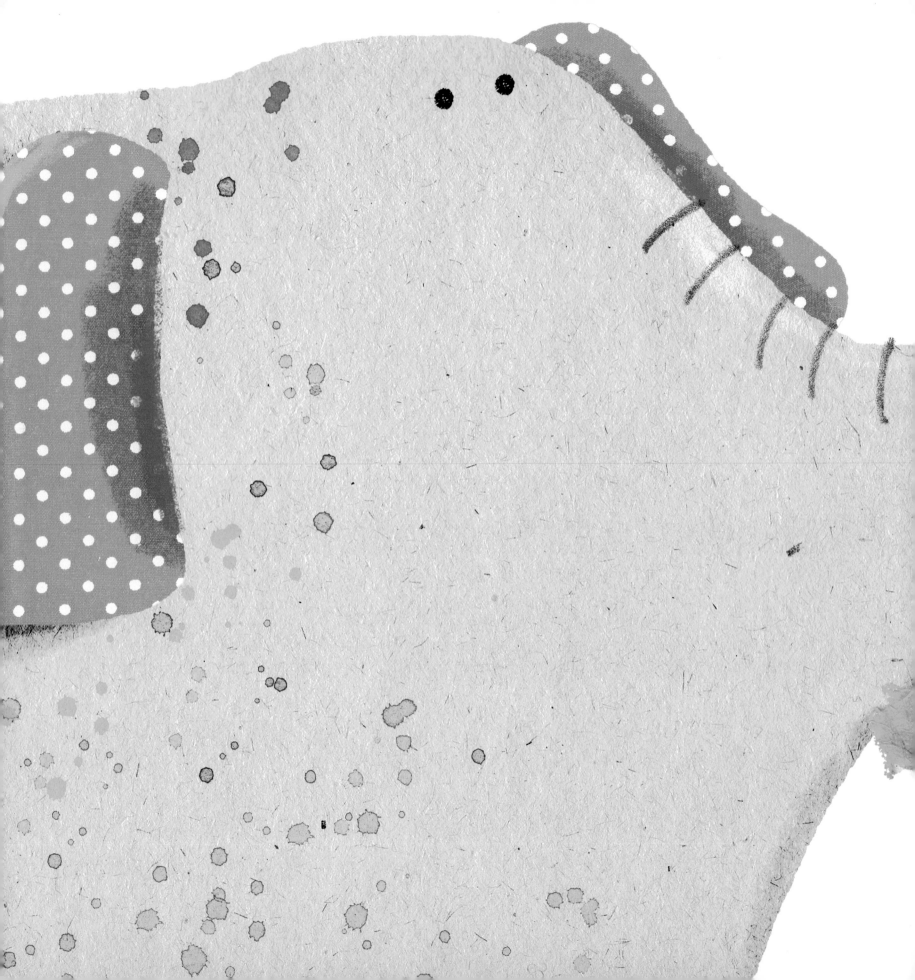

The elephant wrapped his trunk around Ellie's waist and lifted her up.

"Ooh!" said Ellie.

But the elephant took a good long look at her . . .

Then he dropped her on the floor. "Ouch!" said Ellie furiously.

She had a terrible tantrum.

"I don't want **that** elephant," she shouted.
"Get me a different one!"

"But it's an extraordinary elephant," said her father wisely.
"I think it's just the one you need."

So the elephant stayed and made himself at home.
He slept in Ellie's bed.

He wore her best clothes.

He ate her breakfast.

He played with her toys.

"But they're mine!" Ellie howled.

The elephant took no notice. He even went to school and sat in Ellie's place and played with Ellie's friends.

"Go away!" Ellie ordered. But the elephant ignored her.

Now the elephant had everything. Ellie even had to make his sandwiches and clean his boots and fold his handkerchiefs. He didn't say "please" or "thank you."

And if Ellie didn't do exactly what he wanted . . .

eleph

he had an

enormous

antantrum!

Ellie started to cry. The elephant passed her a handkerchief.

"Thank you," said Ellie.
It was the first time she had ever said "thank you."

Then Ellie said,
"Please can I have
my things back?"

"Why don't we share them?"
said the elephant.

"All right," said Ellie happily.
"Let's share."

So they played together and it was **wonderful**.

When they went to school, Ellie said,

"Would you **please** take my friends for a ride in the playground?"

"Of course," said the elephant.

"Thank you," said Ellie.

They all took turns, EVEN Ellie.

It was fun.

It was extraordinary!

That night, Ellie said, "I hope you'll stay forever."

"I can't," said the elephant gently. "There are other children who need me too. You'll have to share me."

Ellie didn't scream or shout or have a tantrum. "I understand," she said.

And when she woke up, the elephant had gone . . .